PL JAN 2016
HD AUG 16
WK DEC 2016
VE MAR 2017

Book #5 in the *Becoming a Better You!* series

Are You Grateful Today?

Written by Kris Yankee and Marian Nelson • Illustrated by Jeff Covieo

This is a work of fiction. Names, characters, places, and incidents either are products of the author's imagination or are used fictitiously. Any resemblance to actual events, locales, or persons, living or dead, is entirely coincidental.

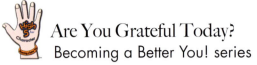

Are You Grateful Today?
Becoming a Better You! series

Copyright © 2015 by Kris Yankee and Marian Nelson

Layout and cover design by Jacqueline L. Challiss Hill
Illustrations by Jeff Covieo
Illustrations created with digital graphics

Printed in Canada

All rights reserved. No part of this publication may be reproduced or transmitted in any form by any means, electronic or mechanical, including photocopy, recording, or any other information storage and retrieval system, without permission in writing from the publisher.

Summary: Kids learn ways to be grateful about themselves and others.
Library of Congress Cataloging-in-Publication Data
Yankee, Kris and Nelson, Marian
Are You Grateful Today?/Kris Yankee and Marian Nelson–First Edition
ISBN-13: 978-1-938326-28-8
1. Gratefulness. 2. Respect. 3. Self-esteem. 4. Character education. 5. Confidence. 6. Appreciation.
I. Yankee, Kris and Nelson, Marian II. Title
Library of Congress Control Number: 2015904003

FERNE PRESS

Ferne Press is an imprint of Nelson Publishing & Marketing
366 Welch Road, Northville, MI 48167
www.nelsonpublishingandmarketing.com
(248) 735-0418

More Praise for *Are You Grateful Today?*

"I learned that sometimes you need to be grateful to others for what they do and give to you. This book shows all the different ways that you can be grateful to others. Other kids should read this book so that they can learn ways to be grateful to everyone." ~Jada C., Nine years old

"What a great message for kids! My favorite parts of the book are the many concrete ideas I can use with my kids and things we can do as a family to teach them this message of gratitude. I also love that the book teaches kids to interact with the world around them in a positive and respectful way when they are surrounded by so many negative messages today." ~Christa Greene, Mother of three children

"I found *Are You Grateful Today?* to carry a powerful message to both the reader and the listener. The book is easy to read and listen to. It defines the term 'grateful' and provides concrete examples of what it is to be grateful. The emphasis on character development and family values is a strong motivator for me to not only purchase the book and share with others but to review the entire series. Finally the *Reflections* and *Tips for Creating Grateful Kids* are an added bonus that will truly strengthen the message of the book and provide practical and rewarding applications." ~Lorna Durand, Educator, Parent, and Grandparent

---

I always wanted to be an artist as a kid. As I grew older, what it meant to be an artist changed. First I wanted to be a puppeteer, then it was a comic book artist, then an animator, a painter, and then a photographer. As those dreams and ideas shifted, I met a lot of very supportive and inspirational people who helped guide me along the way. So, to Jack, Mary, Sharon, Charles, Larry, Lynda, Dave, Sammy, Kris, Marian, Madison, Mark, Donna, Kristi, and most of all Steven...thank you. ~Jeff Covieo

Dedication

This book is dedicated to all of the great role models, parents, educators, and individuals who are committed to building healthy character in people of all ages. It is because of your loyalty to humanity that we will see the lasting results in our children. They will grow up to be positive role models for the next generation.

A special thank you to the staff at Nelson Publishing & Marketing, Kathy Dyer, Amanda Clothier, Jacqueline Hill, and Jennifer Lenders, for their ideas, suggestions, support, and vision for the future.

Every day is a new day.

Today is about being grateful.

When you are grateful, you are a thankful person.
You can show you are grateful by appreciating yourself and others with your actions and words.

Try this!
Each day when you wake up, say out loud,
"I am grateful for my home, family, friends, happiness, and my health."

"Mom and Dad,
I just want to tell you that I love you."

Look around and notice that you have a bed to sleep in,
food to eat, and clothes to wear.
Remind yourself that you are grateful for many things.

Thank your family and caregivers for their love.
Hugs and kisses show you love them, too.

Feed and play with your pet.
You'll know they are grateful when they wag their tails
and cuddle in your lap.

"Here we go, Oreo!"

Hey! You're smart and can learn new things, like reading, math, and how to write stories.
Knowledge will help you make good decisions your whole life.
Be grateful for every time you learn something new.

Thank your teachers for how hard they work to help you learn.

Some people play musical instruments.
Others are great artists.

Find what you are good at
and be grateful for your talents.

Look at yourself in the mirror every day
and appreciate your hair, face, and strong body.

You are fantastic!

Remember, what matters most are your positive thoughts, words, and actions, not what you wear or things you have.

"Thank you for this meal!"

When you work hard,
you will appreciate what you've earned.

Show your friends that you care about them.
You can help others by encouraging them to do their best.

"C'mon, you can do it!"

"Okay.
I will try."

A grateful person listens, cares, and happily shares.

This is YOU!

When you act as a good role model for others, they will be thankful for your leadership.

Your mom or dad will be grateful if you are helpful around the house.
Clean up your room.
Set the table.
Do your chores without being asked.

We feel happy when we work together to accomplish our goals.

Being a team player is important;
it's not just one person who wins for the team.

Grateful people are not selfish.

When each team player gives his or her best effort, the whole team improves.

Decide to start today.
Hug your grandma and grandpa when they help you.

Thank your brother or sister for helping you do your homework.

When you lay your head down
on your pillow tonight,
think about all of the ways you felt grateful
and those times you showed kindness to others.
Practice, practice, and never give up.
Give yourself a big hug.

Reflections

- Make a list of the things you are grateful for and hang it on the refrigerator or on your bedroom door. Look at it each night before you go to sleep. Smile because you know you are a grateful person and you are learning to do the right thing.
- Grateful people are aware of others and look for the good in each other. Name three things you're grateful for in a friend, a family member, and/or a teacher.
- What are some ways you can express your gratitude toward others?
- Sometimes people help you. Name two ways that people have helped you and talk about how that made you feel.
- Make a "Grateful Box." You can use this box two ways: A. Write the names of family members on pieces of paper and put them inside the box. During dinner or another family time, take out one of the slips of paper and tell that person why you are grateful for them. B. Write something that someone did for you or something that you did for another person. During dinner or another family time, share what you've written on the slips or re-read them when you're feeling especially ungrateful.
- Do a "Grateful Challenge" by keeping track of people who have made you feel grateful or times that you felt grateful. Do this for five days and then share with your parents.
- Is a grateful person happier? Why?
- Name five ways you are grateful for your teacher.
- If you want something, but your parents say you have to earn it, what can you do? You'll be more grateful for the item because you've worked so hard for it.
- Name four great things about yourself. These could have something to do with your personality, your talents, or your heart.
- Name a time when you showed good leadership in a team event or after-school activity. Explain what you did.
- Your family is grateful when everyone does his or her share of the work. Name two chores that you do.

Tips for Creating Grateful Kids

- Help kids discover what they are good at by nurturing their interests. Be grateful for their individuality.
- When kids are curious, they tend to learn new things. Answering their questions helps kids feel confident. If you don't have an answer, look it up with your child and you might learn something new, too.
- Encourage kids to work in groups so that they learn to compromise and work toward the goal of the project. By doing this, they will be grateful for the outcome.
- Service-learning projects teach kids that their actions create gratefulness in those whom they are helping. Helping at a food bank or an animal shelter can give kids an immediate response to their efforts.
- Spending time with grandparents or the elderly provides an opportunity to gain wisdom. Teach your kids to be grateful for their stories and memories.
- A person with a truly grateful heart is empathetic to those less fortunate and will want to help. Encourage empathy toward others with your kids by finding organizations in your community and volunteering your time as a family.
- Children who have consistent chores are more organized, confident, and respectful. These traits lead to gratefulness. Having each member do chores represents an integral part of a family working together.
- Gratefulness and empathy are learned behaviors. Set a good example by being grateful and empathetic toward others. Help your kids practice being grateful and empathetic daily.
- Teach your kids not to waste food or other items because parents work hard to be able to provide for each family member. Remind your kids to be grateful for what they've been given.
- When playing on a sports team, your child will be grateful to you when you show the coaches and referees respect. Always set a good and positive example.
- Encourage kids to be patient while waiting for their desires and wants. Delayed gratification is a hard lesson to learn, but by practicing patience, kids will be more grateful. And, you'll be grateful that they've learned how to wait.

Dear Reader,

We want readers to take a new look at the most important things that we have in our lives—our families, our homes, the food on our tables, our warm beds—and realize that these are the things we should be most grateful for each day. Many of us take for granted basic necessities (like food, water, love, shelter) and hold these things as expectations, when really there are many who live in this world without these basics.

In today's society, kids are growing up with 24/7 television and technology that is constantly changing. Advertisers know exactly how to get kids to "want" their goods as necessities and many parents end up getting sucked in. These "wants" aren't necessarily "needs," and this is what can confuse kids. Reminding kids of our basic needs and praising each other for being able to provide for those basic needs (i.e. "Thank you, honey, I'm grateful for your job which provides this meal, home, clothes…for our family.") helps kids realize that the growing feeling in their hearts is gratefulness.

When our hearts are full of love and joy, we can be truly grateful. Our desire for "wants" lessens as we realize that we are satisfied. The newest gadget will only bring a brief moment of joy; the love we hold in our hearts is what sustains us.

Thank you for helping us create character kids.

Kris Yankee and Marian Nelson

Author Biographies

Photo by Eric Yankee

Kris Yankee is the co-founder of High 5 for Character, as well as an editor, writer, and mom. The values presented by High 5 for Character and this new series are those that she and her husband hope to instill in their two children. She is an award-winning author of several titles. Visit krisyankee.com or find Kris on Facebook and Twitter.

For ten years, Marian Nelson has been the publisher for Nelson Publishing & Marketing with over 165 titles in print. As a veteran educator, Marian keeps her focus on the children of the world, actively pursuing concepts that build healthy character. It is her hope that people will continue to learn, grow, and be inspired by all of the books that we publish. Visit nelsonpublishingandmarketing.com to see the wide variety of subject matter.

Photo by Eric Yankee

Visit us at high5forcharacter.com.

Like us at facebook.com/High5ForCharacter   Follow us on Twitter @Hi5ForCharacter

Illustrator Biography

Jeff Covieo has been drawing since he could hold a pencil and hasn't stopped since. He has a BFA in photography from College for Creative Studies in Michigan and works in the commercial photography field, though drawing and illustration have been his avocation for years. *Are You Grateful Today?* is the twelfth book he has illustrated.